The Hippopotamus That Didn't Give Up

Born six weeks premature, Fiona's chance of survival was slim. Thanks to the love and dedication of her caregivers at the Cincinnati Zoo, Fiona survived and thrived against all odds. This is the story of Fiona's perseverance as seen through the eyes and art of second and third grade students from Beach Elementary School in Cedar Springs, Michigan.

The Hippopotamus That Didn't Give Up
by Vicki Burke

Cover layout and interior design by V. Burke

Editing by Renee Waring,
Guardian Proofreading Services

To the dedicated caregivers of Team Fiona who, through trying days and seemingly endless nights, never gave up!

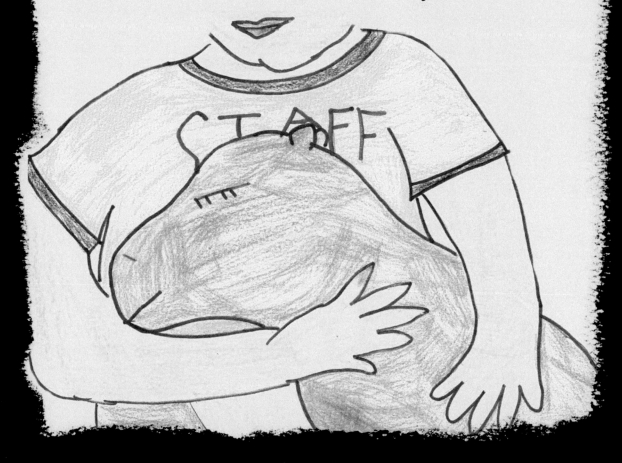

Proceeds from this publication will help support Fiona's care.

For Fiona... ♥

Some thought it was because she was anxious to meet her new friends,

but her caregivers knew that being born early meant every day would be a struggle, learning to do what baby hippos were supposed to do.

Her caregivers loved her,

comforted her,

encouraged her,

and named her Fiona.

Fiona could not eat or drink,

and Fiona could not play with her caregivers, but...

she didn't give up!

Her caregivers helped her to stand and walk, and

each day she tried to swim,

tried to eat and drink,

tried to play,

but mostly she slept.

Fiona's caregivers worried
Fiona was too weak,

but Fiona proved them wrong.

Little by little, while she slept, she grew stronger.

Still, she couldn't stand,

or swim,

13

Or eat,

Or play,

but little Fiona didn't give up!

One day, Fiona took her first wobbly step...

then fell down.

She took a dip in
the pool,

but didn't know
how to float.

She tried to drink from her bottle,

but didn't know how.

She saw bright colored toys around her,

but didn't know how to play.

But little Fiona didn't give up.

The next day she took two wobbly steps...

then another.

In her pool she learned to put her feet down, which helped her nose float above the water.

The bottle was still a little tricky,

and the toys didn't move by themselves,

but little Fiona didn't give up!

Hippo power!

Soon she was walking all around her pen,

Look at me!

and playing with the hose,

It tickles.

and diving
underwater,

and pushing her
toys with her nose.

And the bottle?
She didn't give up.
She learned to eat
from that bottle,

And because she
didn't give up...

Fiona grew,

and grew,

and grew even more,

until she wasn't so little anymore.

Still, she didn't know all the things a hippopotamus should know,

but she didn't give up.

Each day she tried a little harder, until she learned to run around her pen, and swim in an even bigger pool,

30

and eat hay like other hippos,

and even play with her toys.

One day Fiona met her mother and father and she wanted to be big just like them.

So, Fiona ate

and swam,

and grew,

and grew,

and grew even more,

and she knew she couldn't give up.

It wouldn't be long before Fiona was big enough to join her mother and father and the other hippos.

Fiona walked proudly to the large swimming area where she swam like the big hippos,

and ate grain and hay like the other hippos.

Fiona was happy. She smiled a big smile. She was on her way to becoming a real big hippopotamus all because...

Hurray for me!

she didn't give up!

The End